CHANGES

Written by **Marjorie N. Allen** and **Shelley Rotner**

Photographs by **Shelley Rotner**

Macmillan Publishing Company • New York   Collier Macmillan Canada • Toronto

Maxwell Macmillan International Publishing Group • New York   Oxford   Singapore   Sydney

Macmillan Publishing Company
866 Third Avenue, New York, NY 10022
Collier Macmillan Canada, Inc.
1200 Eglinton Avenue East, Suite 200, Don Mills, Ontario M3C 3N1
First edition   Printed and bound in Hong Kong

10   9   8   7   6   5   4   3   2   1

The text of this book is set in 20 point Jensen.
The photographs were taken on 35mm Kodachrome film
and reproduced from color transparencies.

Library of Congress Cataloging-in-Publication Data
Allen, Marjorie N.
Changes / written by Marjorie N. Allen and Shelley Rotner ;
photographs by Shelley Rotner.—1st ed.   p.   cm.
Summary: Describes, in rhymed text and illustrations, how things
in nature change as they grow and develop.
[1. Nature—Fiction.   2. Stories in rhyme.]   I. Rotner, Shelley, ill.
II. Title. PZ8.3.A4192Ch 1991 [E]—dc20 90-6601 CIP AC
ISBN 0-02-700252-7

For Dena with love
—M.N.A.

For Emily and Stephen,
the best changes in my life
—S.R.

All things go through changes

as they grow.

From fiddleheads to uncurled ferns,

scattered pinecones — forest tall;

flowers peek through one last snow

as winter's gray turns to green.

Milkweed clusters bloom in spring;

and feathered seeds in autumn
dance lightly in the wind.

Sun gives way to clouds,
clouds and wind to rain,

and winter's cold brings
ice and snow.

Seasons change —

leaves fall.

Spring blossoms yield summer fruit;

in autumn, corn grows high.

All things change,

then change again.

From fragile eggs

to birds

in flight,

from spotted fawn to great-horned buck,

and piglet small

to giant sow.

Horses, too — foal to mare.

All things

go through changes

as they grow.